The FARTING SANTA

Written and Illustrated by
Charlene Mackesy

ISBN: 978-1-956677-94-2

Let's spend the day with Santa and elves in his workshop!

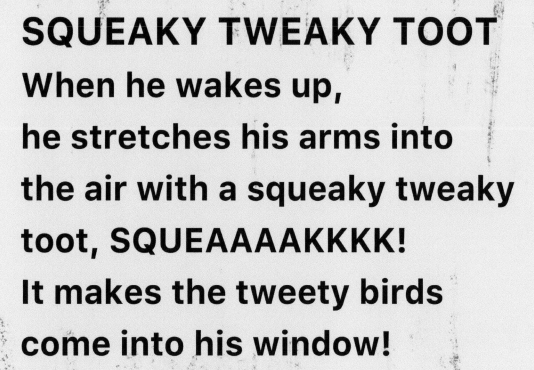

SQUEAKY TWEAKY TOOT

When he wakes up,
he stretches his arms into
the air with a squeaky tweaky
toot, SQUEAAAAKKKK!
It makes the tweety birds
come into his window!

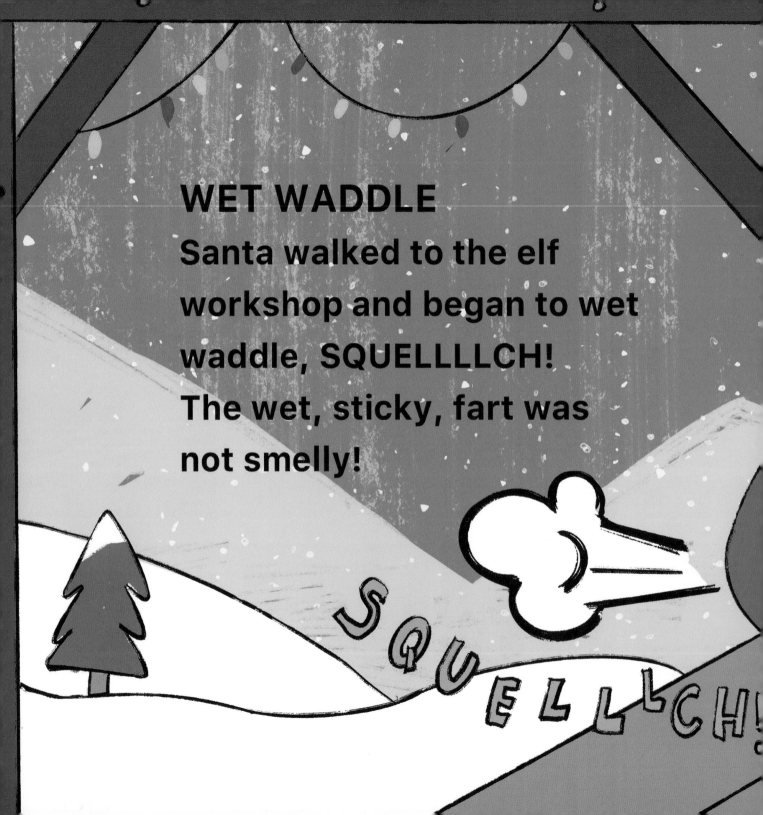

WET WADDLE

Santa walked to the elf workshop and began to wet waddle, SQUELLLLCH! The wet, sticky, fart was not smelly!

RUMBLE RUMP

Santa watched the elves
make toys when,
a rumble rump came,
RRRRUMPP! The ground shook
under the workshop!

SILENT STINKER

Now, Santa walks around the elves to make sure they are doing their jobs, when he lets out a silent stinker. PFFFF.

One sniff of the air
and the elves all fall down!

BOOTY DUTY

Santa needs the elves to keep working, so with all his might, he sneaks out the booty duty, a toot that is so loud, and crazy, it sounds like an alarm!

BURRRAAHH, BURRRAAHH! The loud alarm fart woke up the elves!

FUNKY FLYING FRUMP

Now, it's time to check out
the North Pole. Santa takes
a deep breath and there goes a funky,
flying, frump, FRUUUMMMP!
Santa goes flying up in
the air with a whirlwind,
and hears an elf call for help!

BRROOOSH!

BOOTY BLASTER

This calls for the booty blaster,
BRROOOSH! a green gas
that shoots out of his booty
and makes him fly fast!
Santa flies to help the elf.

SIZZLER FIZZLER

To melt a marshmallow, you need heat. He uses his Sizzler Fizzler, A fart that sizzles anything, FRIZZZZZ! The marshmallow melts, yay!

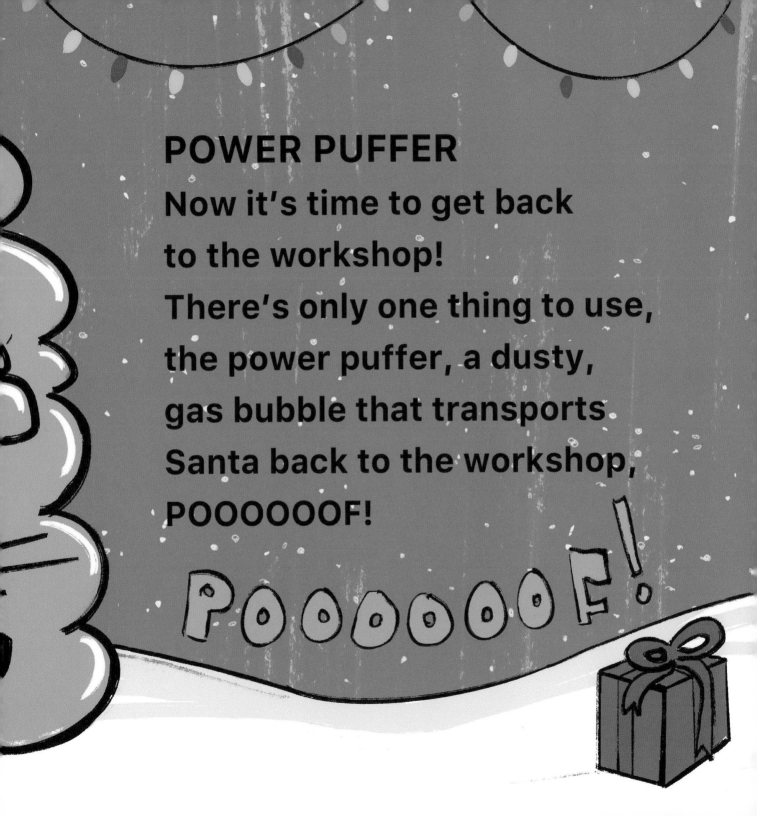

POWER PUFFER

Now it's time to get back
to the workshop!
There's only one thing to use,
the power puffer, a dusty,
gas bubble that transports
Santa back to the workshop,
POOOOOOF!

POOOOOOF!

BOOTY BLINDER

The bubble was so strong,
no one could see!
That is also known as
the booty blinder, PFFFFFT!

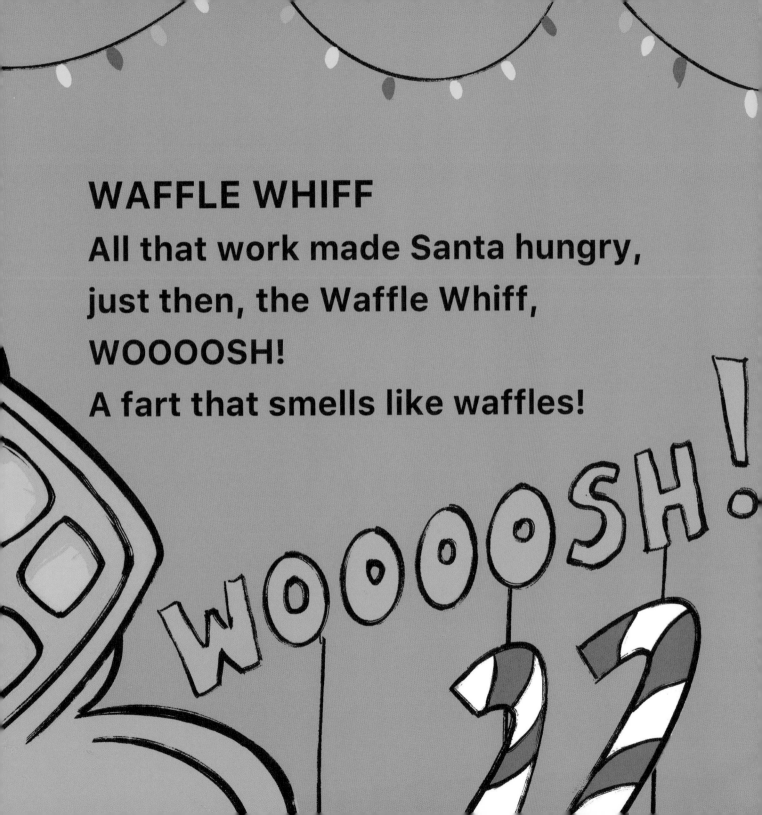

WAFFLE WHIFF

All that work made Santa hungry,
just then, the Waffle Whiff,
WOOOOSH!
A fart that smells like waffles!

DUSTY CRUSTY

Santa says goodbye to the elves,
he does a Dusty Crusty, POOOOT!

THUNDER TRUMP, A RIPPLE RUMBLE

When Santa goes back to
his bed for a good night,
he does a thunder trump,
a Ripple Rumble, RRRRRUMBLE,
TRUUUMPP, It shakes his bed
and throws his blankets on him.

Goodnight! BRRRRAP!

BRRRRAP!

THANKS FOR PURCHASING OUR
FARTING STORIES
TAKE OUT A LITTLE TIME TO RATE
US ON AMAZON
IT WILL BE SO MUCH APPRECIATED

Printed in Great Britain
by Amazon